I AM READING

Scratching's Catching!

JANE CLARKE

ILLUSTRATED BY

JAN LEWIS

KINGFISHER

BOSTON

KINGFISHER
a Houghton Mifflin Company imprint
222 Berkeley Street
Boston, Massachusetts 02116
www.houghtonmifflinbooks.com

First published in 2007
2 4 6 8 10 9 7 5 3 1

LIBRARY OF CONGRESS CATALOGING-IN-PUBLICATION DATA
has been applied for.

ISBN-13: 978-0-7534-5958-4

Printed in China
1TR/0107/WKT/SCHOY/140MA/C

Contents

Chapter One

In the peaceful kingdom of Hairia,
everyone was busy growing their hair.
Princess Primrose rushed into the
palace. She pushed her long, long hair
out of her eyes.

"Daddy!" she squeaked. "It's in the
newspaper! The kingdom of Hairia
is lousy!"

"Don't you believe it, princess," said the king, strumming his guitar. "Hairia is a great kingdom!"

"Not that sort of lousy! Lousy with itchy head lice!" Princess Primrose told him. "I might catch them! You might catch them too!"

The king pushed his long hair out of his eyes. "Itchy lice here, itchy lice there, get those head lice out of my hair," he sang.

"Stop singing and do something, Daddy!" Primrose said.

The king took off his dark glasses and
put down his guitar.

"No problem, princess," he said.

The king went out onto the balcony of the palace. The crowd below looked like a sea of hair. Two or three people were scratching their heads.

The king spoke into the microphone. "Everyone must wash their hair!" he announced. "No lice in the kingdom of Hairia!"

The crowd gulped. No one in Hairia liked washing their long, long hair.

Chapter Two

Ouch! Ouch! Ouch!

For days, the kingdom of Hairia rang with cries of "Ouch!" as shampoo got in everyone's eyes. The sky over Hairia was full of bubbles. But it was no use.

"Head lice like clean hair!" Princess
Primrose said. "They're spreading."

The king strummed his guitar.

"It's not a dream, lice like it clean," he sang.

"Stop singing!" Princess Primrose wailed. "I might catch them! You might catch them! Do something, Daddy!"

"No problem, princess," said the king.

The king went out onto the balcony of the palace. The crowd below looked like a sea of hair and hands. Half of the people were scratching their heads.

The king took the microphone in one hand and held up a hairbrush in his other hand.

"This is the only hairbrush in the kingdom of Hairia!" he announced. "Everyone must brush their hair with it! No lice in the kingdom of Hairia!"

The crowd muttered. No one in Hairia ever brushed their hair.

Oww! Owww!
OwwwWw!
For days, the
kingdom of Hairia
rang with cries of
"Owww!" as people
dragged the hairbrush
through their hair.
But it was no use.

"Head lice like people to share a hairbrush!" Princess Primrose said. "They're spreading!"

"Never share when you brush your hair," sang the king, strumming his guitar.

"I might catch them! You might catch them!" Princess Primrose cried. "Stop singing and do something, Daddy!"

"No problem, princess," said the king.

Chapter Three

From the balcony of the palace, the
crowd below looked like a field of
fidgety fingers. Everyone was scratching.
The king spoke into the microphone.
"No more scratching!" he announced.

"Everyone must cut their hair!"

The crowd gasped.

No one in Hairia ever cut their hair.

The gasp
turned into
a mumble,

the mumble
turned into
a mutter,

and the mutter
turned into
a roar.

"Do something, Daddy!" Princess Primrose yelled.

"No problem, princess," said the king.

"Send for the scissors!"

The king cut his hair right there and then and called for his guitar.

"No lice today, my hair has gone away," he sang.

"Cool!" gasped the crowd.

For days, the kingdom of Hairia rang with cries of "Cool!" as the people cut their hair. The streets of Hairia were ankle-deep in hair.

"No Lice Today" reached number one on the music charts.

"No Scratching" signs were put up everywhere.

"That's it!" said the king at last.
"There are no more lice in Hairia."
"Phew!" said Princess Primrose,
combing her long, long hair. "Thank
goodness I didn't catch head lice."
But lice take a while to hatch . . .

Chapter Four

The king and the princess went out onto the balcony of the palace. The crowd below was admiring each other's new haircuts. The royal trumpeters trumpeted. There was a drumroll.

The king took the microphone.

"There are no lice in the kingdom of Hairia!" he announced.

"Hooray!" cheered the crowd.

The king strummed his guitar.

Everyone joined in singing "No Lice Today." "No more scratching, scratching's catching," they sang.

At that very moment, Princess
Primrose felt something.
Something moved in her long, long
hair—something itchy.

She scratched her head.

The crowd stopped singing.

Princess Primrose continued scratching her head.

"No more scratching, scratching's catching!" the crowd sang, scratching their heads.

"She's got lice!" someone screeched.

"Lice! Lice! Lice!" the crowd roared.

"Do something, Daddy!" shrieked Princess Primrose.

The king checked out Primrose's head.

"Your hair's crawling with head lice, and there are lots more waiting to hatch!" he whispered.

"Off with her hair! Off with her hair! Off with her hair!" chanted the crowd.

"This is a problem, princess," said the king.

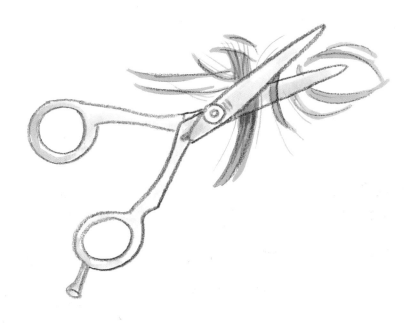

Chapter Five

"Off with her hair!" the crowd shouted over and over again.

"Send for the scissors," said the king.

Princess Primrose closed her eyes.

"I wish I didn't have lice!" she cried.

"I wish I could keep my long, long hair!"

Pffffff!

A very hairy fairy with a mustache and a beard appeared in a puff of smoke. "Wow!" gasped the crowd.

"Who are you?" the princess asked with a sniffle.

"I am your Hairy Godmother," said the hairy fairy. "I will grant your wish."

Princess Primrose's Hairy Godmother
waved her wand. A comb flew into
her hand.

"Lice are no problem!" she said. "You can keep your long, long hair. Just wash it, condition it, and comb it again and again and again with this special comb."

She twirled her wand once more.
A bottle flew into her hand.

"Or use this bottle of special shampoo and comb your hair with the special comb again . . ."

". . . and again and again?" asked Princess Primrose.

"That's right!" said the Hairy Godmother, twirling her mustache. "And don't share brushes, combs, or hats!"

Pfffffff!

And she disappeared in another puff of smoke.

Chapter Six

The king put on his dark glasses and spoke into the microphone.

"Now that we know what to do if we get lice, we can grow our hair long again!" he announced.

He strummed his guitar. "Lice aren't our problem anymore, let's grow our hair down to the floor!" he sang.

The crowd went wild.

Princess Primrose scratched her head. "I have the longest hair in Hairia," she said. "All that combing again and again and again is too much trouble. Stop singing and do something, Daddy!"

The king took out the scissors,

shampoo, and comb.

"No problem, princess," he said.

The king sent for a mirror so that Princess Primrose could see her short, spiky hair.

HAIR WE GROW

"It's great!" Primrose said. "From now on, I will have the shortest hair in Hairia! Thank you, Daddy!"

"No problem, princess," said the king.

So Princess Primrose kept her hair short, while the king and all the people of Hairia grew their hair long again.

And they all lived happily ever after,

as you'd expect from a hairy story . . .

unless it's a lousy one, of course!

About the author and illustrator

Jane Clarke has been an archaeologist, a teacher, and a library assistant, but she likes being a writer best of all. She started to make up stories when her sons were small, but she didn't write anything down until they were big and hairy. Since then, she's been itching to write a hairy story.

Jan Lewis lives in southern England with her two large sons and two small dogs. Sometimes her hair does very strange things in the morning, but luckily she has never had lice. Her two sons did when they were little, though, so Jan knows all about combs and conditioners.

Strategies for Independent Readers

Predict

Think about the cover, illustrations, and the title of the book. What do you think this book will be about? While you are reading think about what may happen next and why.

Monitor

As you read ask yourself if what you're reading makes sense. If it doesn't, reread, look at the illustrations, or read ahead.

Question

Ask yourself questions about important ideas in the story such as what the characters might do or what you might learn.

Phonics

If there is a word that you do not know, look carefully at the letters, sounds, and word parts that you do know. Blend the sounds to read the word. Ask yourself if this is a word you know. Does it make sense in the sentence?

Summarize

Think about the characters, the setting where the story takes place, and the problem the characters faced in the story. Tell the important ideas in the beginning, middle, and end of the story.

Evaluate

Ask yourself questions like: Did you like the story? Why or why not? How did the author make the story come alive? How did the author make the story fun to read? How well did you understand the story? Maybe you can understand it better if you read it again!